Our Five Senses

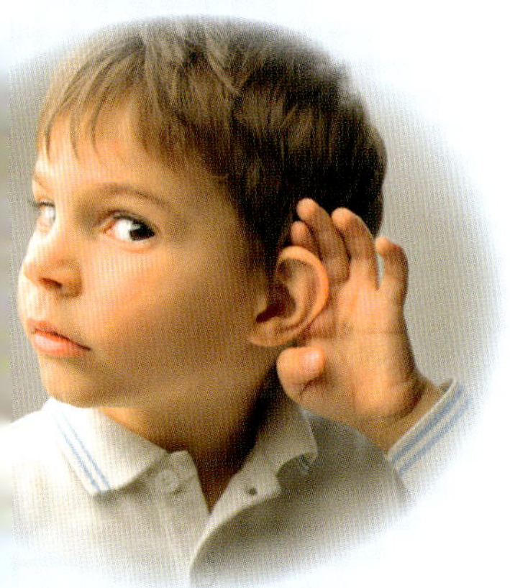

Sarah Russell

Contents

Our Senses

We have five senses.
We can see, hear, smell,
taste and feel.

We need our senses.
They help us to **learn**.
They help us to stay safe.

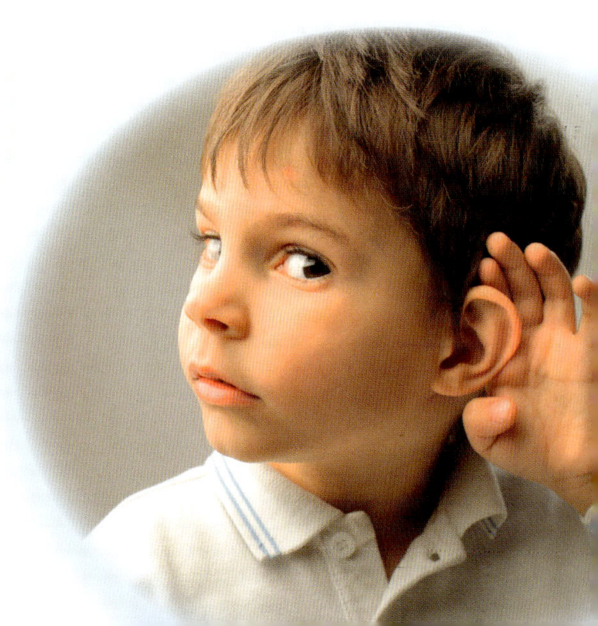

Our Eyes

We see with our eyes.
We see lots of things around us.

Our eyes help us to read the words in our books.

Our eyes help us to see the colours of a rainbow.

We can see when it is safe to walk across a road.

Our Ears

We hear with our ears.
We can hear lots of things around us.

Our ears help us to hear rain
falling on the roof.

Our ears help us to hear the music
to a new song.

We can hear if a big dog barks at us.

Our Noses

We smell with our noses.
We can smell lots of things around us.

Our noses help us to smell flowers in the garden.

Our noses help us to smell smoke
if there is a fire.

We can smell the sea
when we are playing at the beach.

Our Tongues

We taste with our tongues.
We can taste lots of things.

Our tongues help us to taste ice cream.

Our tongues can help us to taste things that could make us sick.

Our Skin

We feel with our **skin**.
We can feel lots of things.

The skin on our hands
helps us to feel sand and water.

The skin on our arms and legs
feels hot if we stay out in the sun
for too long.

Our skin can feel cold
when we are playing out in the snow.

Learning and Staying Safe

We need each one of our five senses.

They help us to learn
and to stay safe every day.

Glossary

learn to find out

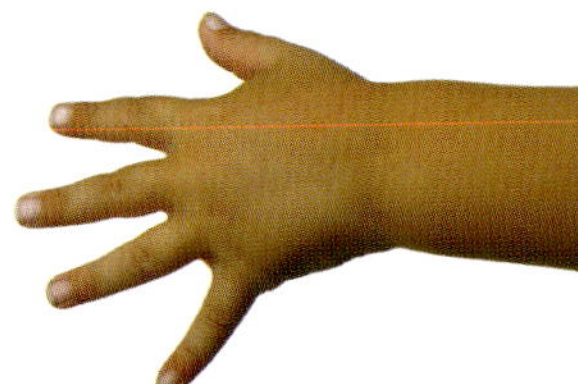

skin the thin cover over our bodies

taste to feel something good or bad in our mouths